WALT DISNEY PRODUCTIONS
presents

Goofy Minds the House

Random House New York

BOOK CLUB EDITION

Copyright © 1975 by Walt Disney Productions. All rights reserved under
International and Pan-American Copyright Conventions. Published in the
United States by Random House, Inc., New York, and simultaneously in
Canada by Random House of Canada Limited, Toronto.
Library of Congress Cataloging in Publication Data
Walt Disney Productions presents Goofy minds the house. (Disney's won-
derful world of reading, #31) In this retelling of a Norwegian folktale,
Goofy learns that minding the house is harder than he thought when he
and his wife swap jobs for one day. [1. Folklore—Norway] I. Disney
(Walt) Productions. II. Title: Goofy minds the house. PZ8.1.W18
[E]   75-5851 ISBN 0-394-82573-X   ISBN 0-394-92573-4 (lib. bdg.)
Manufactured in the United States of America   1 2 3 4 5 6 7 8 9 0

A   B   C   D   E   F   G   H   I   J   K
5 6 7 8 9

B

There once was a farmer named Goofy.
He lived in a little house with his wife
and Junior, their son.

Goofy worked in the wheat fields all day,
while his wife stayed home to mind the house.

Every night, when Goofy came home,
he would begin to grumble.

"All I do is work, work, work!
I never have any fun!"

Every night his wife would answer,
"Do you think housework is fun?
I work *much* harder than you do!"

One night Junior said, "If you want to know
whose work is harder, why not change places?"
Goofy and his wife looked at him.
"That's a good idea," they said.

The very next morning
Goofy's wife went out to
work in the fields.
Goofy stayed home
to mind the house.

As soon as his wife was gone,
Goofy put on Junior's roller skates.
"Housework can be fun," he said.
"Just watch how I do it."

Goofy grabbed a broom
and began to sweep
the floor.

He skated from room to room,
sweeping the dust ahead of him.

When he was done, he piled all the dust into one corner.

Junior clapped his hands.
"Take a bow, Dad," he said.

Goofy took a bow.
But his broom caught
in the laundry basket.
Up went the basket.
Down came the clothes—
right into the pile of dust.

"Don't worry, son,"
said Goofy. "I know
just what to do."
He carried the dirty
clothes out to the line.

"Mom always WASHES the clothes before
she hangs them up," said Junior.
"That's the hard way," said Goofy.
"Watch how I do it!"

Goofy hung the clothes
on the line and poured
soap powder all over them.
Then he turned on the hose.

"I'm washing the clothes and giving you
a shower at the same time," said Goofy.

"Yes, Dad!" said Junior.

"But the yard is getting muddy."

Suddenly the cow began to moo.
She sounded very unhappy.
"I forgot to milk the cow!" cried Goofy.

He grabbed a bucket and
ran through the mud.
Then he sat down and
milked the cow.

When Goofy brought the milk into the house,
Junior and the cat came with him.

"Dad!" cried Junior as he pointed
at the floor. "We tracked mud
all over the kitchen."

Goofy looked at the floor.

"Don't worry, son," he said.
"I know just what to do."

Goofy dipped two big sponges
into a bucket of soapy water.
Then he tied the sponges
onto his feet.

Goofy sloshed around the room
mopping up the floor.

"Wasn't that easy?" asked Goofy.

"The mud is gone, Dad," said Junior.
"But what about all the puddles?"

Goofy knew just what to do.

He took out the fan and set it down on the floor.

"Watch this!" he said.

While Goofy was plugging in the fan,
the cat climbed up on the milk pail.

"The cat will knock over the pail!" cried Junior.
"I'll soon stop that," said Goofy.

He grabbed the cat and stuck it
under the laundry basket.

Then Goofy started the fan.

"The breeze will dry those puddles in no time," he said.

But the breeze from the fan blew into the fireplace.

And the ashes from the fireplace
flew right up the chimney.

Junior was looking out the window.

"Dad!" he shouted. "Come here quick!"

Goofy started toward the window.
But he did not look where he was going.
CLUNK went his foot.
CLANG went the pail.
The milk spilled all over the floor.

"I know how to
get rid of that milk,"
said Goofy.

He lifted the basket and let out the cat.
It began to lap up the milk.

Then Goofy ran to the window to see
what Junior was shouting about.

The fan had blown ashes all over the clothes.
The water from the hose had flooded
the yard, so the poor cow was standing
in soapsuds up to her neck.

"Don't worry, son," said Goofy.
"I will take care of the cow!"

Goofy grabbed a long board.
He put it against the house.
Then he pushed the cow
onto the roof.

Now she was safe on top of the house.

"Your mother will soon be home," said Goofy.
"I must go in to cook our dinner."
"I'll watch the cow," said Junior.

Goofy went into the kitchen and
filled the cooking pot with water.

He poured a whole
box of oatmeal into the pot.

Suddenly Junior was shouting.

"Dad!" cried Junior. "The cow
is sliding off the roof."
Goofy looked out the window.
"Don't worry, son," he said.
"We can take care of that."

Goofy pulled the cow back onto the roof.

He took a long rope and tied one end
around her.

He dropped the other end of the rope
down the chimney.

Then Goofy went inside and grabbed
the rope that hung down the chimney.
He tied it around his waist.
"If the cow falls again,"
thought Goofy,
"I'll know about it."

All of a sudden the rope yanked
Goofy right off his feet!
Before he knew what had happened,
he was stuck inside the chimney.
The cow had fallen off the roof again!

Just at that moment, Goofy's wife came home.
She was hot and tired and ready for dinner.

When she looked at the mess,
she could not believe her eyes.
Then she saw the cow!

She ran to the house and cut the rope.
The cow landed safely on the ground.

Goofy slid down the chimney and
splashed into the cooking pot.

Goofy's wife ran into the house.
There was Goofy—up to his ears
in cold oatmeal!

That night Goofy decided that
minding the house was hard work.
His wife decided that working
in the fields was hard, too.

And as for Junior—he was happy.
He didn't hear one more word
about whose work was harder.